THE SPRING Book

TODD PARR

Megan Tingley Books
LITTLE, BROWN AND COMPANY
NEW YORK BOSTON

I am dedicating this book to the world! In hopes that we can all work together to make everyone feel loved and respected.

Love,
Todd

Also by Todd Parr

   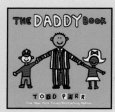  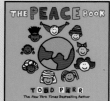

A complete list of Todd's books and more information can be found at toddparr.com.

About This Book

The illustrations for this book were created on a drawing tablet using an iMac, starting with bold black lines and dropping in color with Adobe Photoshop. This book was edited by Megan Tingley and Esther Cajahuaringa and designed by Lynn El-Roeiy. The production was supervised by Bernadette Flinn, and the production editor was Marisa Finkelstein. The text was set in Todd Parr's signature font.

Every day the weather is different.

Rainy

Snowy

Windy

Sunny

Trees are blooming.

Everything is turning green.

And change is in the air.

Spring is here! The birds are singing.

Babies are being born.

We are cleaning out our closets.

And planting gardens.

Everyone is sneezing—

ACHOO!

Spring is the time of year to learn new things.

OKAY! well then, I'm going to stop writing this book, and I'm going to open my first restaurant, TACO TODD'S.

The End. Love, Todd

Surprise! April Fools'!
Don't worry, this story is not over yet.

Spring is a time to dance in the rain.

Celebrate traditions with family and friends.

Play hide-and-seek.

THE

EARTH!

Spring is a time for festivals.

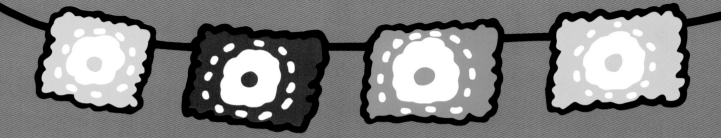

¡De colores se visten los campos en la primavera!

Eating fresh fruits and vegetables.

Having picnics.

Hugging moms on Mother's Day
(and every day).

And honoring heroes.

Now go roll down some hills! Happy spring!